This book belongs to:

For

Mrs. Cruz

From

PTO

SCHOLASTIC

TAILS FROM THE PANTRY

• Little Life Lessons from Mom and Dad •

5 CHEESY STORIES

**About Friendship, Bravery,
Bullying, and More**

By Patsy Clairmont

Illustrated by Joni Oeltjenbruns

THOMAS NELSON

Since 1798

NASHVILLE   DALLAS   MEXICO CITY   RIO DE JANEIRO   BEIJING

Published in Nashville, Tennessee, by Thomas Nelson, Inc., P.O. Box 141000, Nashville, Tennessee, 37214.

Thomas Nelson, Inc., books may be purchased in bulk for educational, business, fundraising, or sales promotional use. For information, please e-mail SpecialMarkets@ThomasNelson.com.

ISBN 10: 1-4003-1042-3
ISBN 13: 978-1-4003-1042-5

Printed in China
07 08 09 10 11 RRD 5 4 3 2

This little series is dedicated to
Justin and Noah. . . .

How blessed I am to have two "little mouse" grandsons who regularly nibble in my pantry. Darlings, leave all the crumbs you want in Nana's house. I'll tidy up later. Always heed Mommy and Daddy's lessons about staying safe. You are both loved "a bushel and a peck and a hug around the neck."

~Nana

TAILS FROM THE PANTRY

· Little Life Lessons from Mom and Dad ·

SOCCER

*O*nce upon a jar of olives sat a mouse named Soccer MacKenzie. Yes, Soccer. His dad, Mac, named him after his favorite sport.

His mom, Lily, told Soccer, "Your dad almost named you after his favorite tool—a wrench."

Soccer thought about that for a minute and decided he really liked his name.

Soccer was practicing jumping, which is why he was perched atop the macaroni in the kitchen pantry. He had hopped onto a sardine can, then shot up onto the pork 'n' beans, and from there hoisted himself up the box of macaroni.

Once there, Soccer sat for a moment to catch his breath, and then as fast as he could, he ran right off the edge of the box. Down, down, down he tumbled, landing on a bag of marshmallows.

Soccer giggled so hard that he began to hiccup. His mom had taught him to hold his breath and count to ten when he had the hiccups. So he took a deep breath. . . .

One, two, three, four, five, six . . . was as high as Soccer could count without taking a breath. But it worked. His hiccups stopped. "Hooray!" Soccer shouted.

"You wouldn't be so happy if you knew what I know," sang a familiar voice.

Soccer looked up and saw Tipsy, the spider, dangling from a silver thread. Tipsy lived in a fancy, spun house behind a jelly jar on the top shelf. Soccer counted on Tipsy to bring him news from outside the pantry they lived in. Soccer wasn't allowed to leave the pantry because of Duff, the old calico cat, who prowled around the house searching for mouse snacks.

"What do you know that I don't know?"
Soccer asked.

"There's a new cat in the house!"
Tipsy announced.

"Is Duff gone?" Soccer asked, puzzled.

"Nooo, now there are TWO cats!"

"Oh my!" Soccer's eyes got really big.
"Two cats?"

"Yep, one, two . . . and guess what else? The
new one's name is Whomp, and I heard he's a
WILD cat."

"Whomp? Wild?" Soccer's knees wobbled. "Did you *see* Whomp?"

"No, Chatter, the ladybug, told me about him."

"Did Chatter see Whomp?"

"Uh . . . well, no, but she *heard* about him from Speck, the housefly, who saw him with her own seven eyes."

"I'd better go and tell my family," Soccer said, scrambling toward home.

Soccer lived in a forgotten box of Christmas candy with his family. Soccer's room was right next to a chocolate-covered caramel, which he loved to nibble on.

When Soccer got home, his mom was washing clothes. After hearing the news, she said, "Soccer, yes, we must be careful whenever we go out, but we also must be careful not to believe everything we hear."

Soccer was supposed to meet Tipsy in half an hour to play a game of checkers, but Soccer didn't know if he wanted to now. He felt scared. Wild cats are fierce and fast.

Then Soccer had an idea. He ran to his toy chest and pulled out his bike helmet, boxing gloves, winter boots, and wooden sword. After putting on his gear, he headed out to meet Tipsy.

Climbing was a bit difficult with boots and boxing gloves, but Soccer inched along carefully.
Suddenly, he tripped and fell backward, helmet
over boots . . . down, down, down, until he land-
ed on a sack of potatoes on the floor. Just then,
he heard a strange sound, and before he could
pick up his sword, a ball of fur with whiskers was
in his face.

"Eeeek!" shrieked Soccer.

"Eeeek!" shrieked the tiny ball of fur. And then
the fur ball began to hiccup. *HIC!*

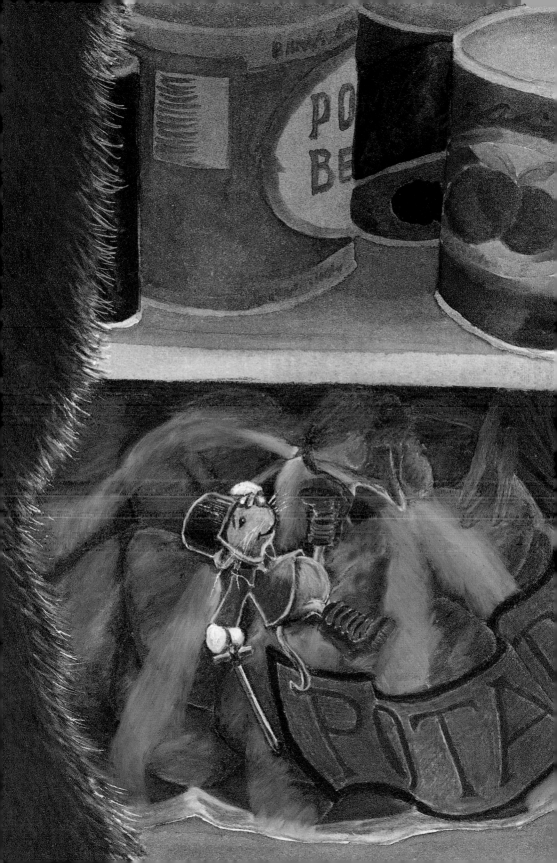

Soccer grabbed his sword and, shaking, yelled, "Who goes there?"

A little voice mewed, "My name is Whomp. Please—**HIC**—don't stick me with your sword."

"*You're* Whomp?" Soccer said. "You're a baby kitten!"

"I'm no baby! I'm just—**HIC**—small for my size. And you are a very oddly dressed mouse. Are you going to—**HIC**—hurt me?" Whomp asked.

"Uh, well, I suppose not. Are you going to smack me with your paw?" questioned Soccer.

"Oh, no, I don't like—**HIC**—hitting," confessed Whomp.

"Whomp," Soccer said as he carefully leaned toward the intruder, "if you hold your breath and count to ten your hiccups will go away."

"Really? Okay." Whomp counted until his cheeks filled with air—one, two, three—and then he gasped.

"My hiccups are gone. Wow! Thanks. Want to be friends?" Whomp asked.

"Friends? I will have to ask my parents about that, but thank you for offering. I have to go home now," Soccer announced.

Soccer took off his boots, tied the shoelaces together, threw the shoes over his shoulder, and dashed for home.

"Mom! Mom!" Soccer called as he ran in the front door. "I fell down and Whomp jumped at me. Whomp is a kitty. Just a baby, Mom. He's not wild at all. You were right. We can't believe everything we hear. Whomp wants to be friends. Can we, Mom? Can we?"

"Calm down, Soccer," his mom told him. "Friends with a cat?"

"He's just a kitty, and he doesn't like hitting."

"Hmm, we'll talk about this when Daddy gets home."

Just then the doorbell rang. It was Tipsy.

"I'm sorry I didn't make it for checkers, Tipsy," Soccer apologized.

"That's okay. I had a delay too," Tipsy admitted. "Chatter came by to say she had misunderstood Speck. Speck didn't say *wild* cat—she said *mild* cat. It turns out, Whomp's a quiet kitty."

"Well," Tipsy continued, "it's like my Aunt Centipede always says, 'You can't believe everything you hear.'"

Soccer just grinned.

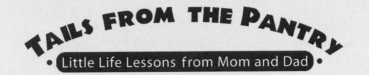

Meatball

*O*nce upon a can of spaghetti sat a mouse named Meatball MacKenzie. Yes, Meatball. Her daddy, Mac, named her after his favorite snack.

"It could have been worse," her mother, Lily, admitted. "He almost named you after his favorite cheese—Limburger."

Lily, thinking her daughter's name was not very girly, painted Meatball's toenails powder puff pink and painted polka dots on her daughter's naturally curly tail.

Meatball liked to practice climbing, which was why she was perched atop the spaghetti can on a shelf in the pantry.

As she was looking around the kitchen, she spotted Duff, the Calico cat. Duff seemed to be the size of an 18-wheeler to Meatball. So when he dropped down on his haunches and began inching across the floor in her direction, Meatball knew she was in trouble.

Meatball jumped from the spaghetti can down onto a can of tuna fish and from there, slid down onto a jar of pears. Without pausing, she darted behind a chubby bag of flour.

Just then Duff, who was now inside the pantry, swatted his furry paw at Meatball's polka dotted tail. But instead of hitting Meatball, Duff smacked the side of the flour bag, causing a great white cloud.

When the air cleared, Duff had flour in his eyes and up his freckled nose. Duff sneezed . . .

ah-choo,

ah-ah-choo,

ah-ah-ah-choo . . .

three times.

That last sneeze was a doozy, throwing Duff backward out of the pantry.

Meatball was coated in flour from her nose to her toes. She spotted an open box of cornflakes on the shelf below her, and when Duff sneezed for the third time, Meatball jumped into the cereal box. Then she burrowed deep into the flakes and lay very still.

Meatball's heart was thumping wildly with fear, but she didn't let out a squeak.

Meatball remembered her mother's safety rules against all cats, misguided bats, and bully rats:

1. Scurry to safety.
2. Be still.
3. Wait patiently.

Meatball waited and waited and waited. In fact, she waited so long she fell fast asleep. When she woke up, all was quiet. Certain Duff was curled up somewhere napping, Meatball decided it was time to venture out of the cereal box.

Meatball wanted to scamper home, which was three shelves up where she lived in a forgotten box of Christmas candy with her family. Her bedroom was right next to a chocolate-covered cherry that she'd been nibbling on for months. Oh, how yummy that sounded right now to her growling tummy!

Meatball crawled on top of the cornflakes and looked up, up, up, to the top of the box. "Oh dear, how am I going to get out of here?" she said out loud.

Meatball tried jumping, but she couldn't jump high enough. And the harder she tried, the more afraid she became. Then she remembered her dad's words: *Think before you jump.* So, Meatball sat down on the cornflakes to think.

Meatball decided to wiggle around to see if there was another way out. She was about to give up when she bumped into something that wasn't a cornflake. It wasn't food of any kind, and it wasn't cardboard like the box. It was something hard, and it made a crinkly sound when she stepped on it.

"Hmmm . . ." Meatball carefully nibbled at the plastic wrap until she could see what was inside. It was a prize—a whistle!

Meatball dragged the whistle to the top of the flakes and then gave it a toot, hoping her family would hear and come to her rescue. She was certain they must be out looking for her.

Tweet, Tweet, Tweet.

She blew on the whistle again and again.

Tweet, Tweet, Tweet.

Then she heard someone call her name.

"Meatball! Meatball!" It was her dad.

"Here, Daddy, here! Inside the cornflakes!"

Peering down into the box, her daddy shouted, "Oh, my little Meatball! You're safe!" Never had her name sounded so wonderful to her little ears.

"We'll get you out," he promised, "but you must do as I say. Dig your way into the center of the cereal and roll up into a ball. Your mom, brother, and I will tip the box over so you can climb out."

"But, Daddy, I'm scared."

"Yes, I know. Being scared is okay, Meatball. Feeling afraid doesn't have to keep you from being brave. So hurry now."

Meatball dug her way into the flakes and tucked herself into a furry ball. Within moments, she felt the box tipping back and forth, back and forth. And down it went onto the shelf. Meatball could feel herself tumbling, and the next thing she knew, she rolled right out of the box!

"Hooray!" they all cheered.

Meatball and her family had a happy reunion, and to celebrate, they feasted on—what else?—spaghetti! What better way is there to celebrate a Meatball?

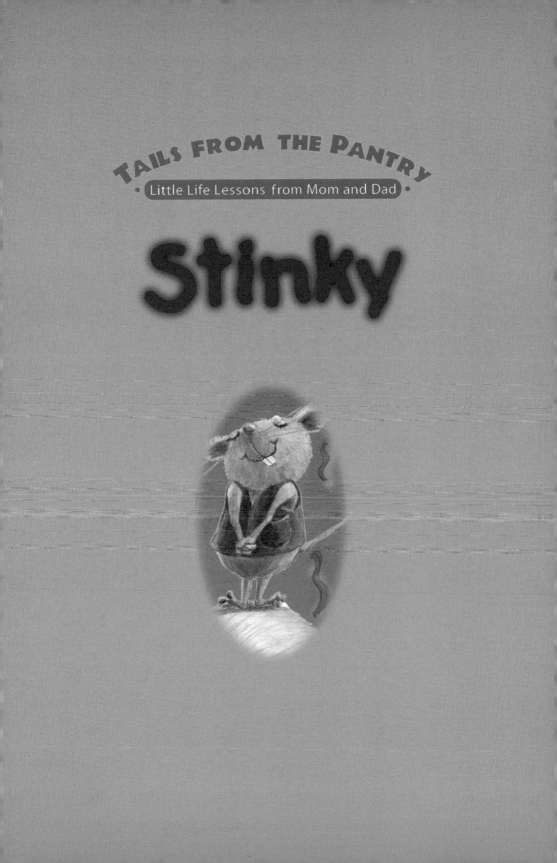

TAILS FROM THE PANTRY

· Little Life Lessons from Mom and Dad ·

Stinky

Once upon a can of sardines sat a mouse named Stinky. Yes, Stinky. His real name, Stephanopolous, seemed to be a lot of letters for a tiny mouse to tote around. And because Stephanopolous loved to gnaw on garlic cloves and nibble onions, he was nicknamed Stinky. He was actually quite proud of his nickname. Stinky thought his name fragrant.

Stinky's mom, Lily, told Stinky that his dad, Mac, almost named him after his favorite hat—fedora. Stinky didn't think *fedora* fit him. Luckily, Mac decided to name his son after his favorite brother, Stephanopolous Metropolis. Stinky lived in the pantry in a forgotten box of Christmas candy with his family.

One morning Stinky was sitting atop the sardine can, awaiting his friends Tid and Bit. Tid and Bit, ants from the baseboard colony, loved to ride in Stinky's vest pocket. It was better than a roller coaster when Stinky jumped from can to can in the pantry.

Up, up

they'd go . . . then

down,
       down

they'd come until they reached their favorite spot that they visited every week. Tid and Bit would scurry out of their friend's pocket and head right for the sugar granules at the base of the canister, while Stinky made his way to the bag of garlic cloves for a nibble.

But their friendship hadn't always been such a fun ride. When Tid and Bit first met Stinky, he was mindlessly slurping on an onion. After one especially large slurp, something suddenly stung Stinky's foot. "Ouch!" he cried.

Stinky looked down. There was a broom straw sticking out of his big toe, and beside his foot was Bit yelling up at him, "Don't swallow! You lapped up my brother! He's on your tongue!"

Puzzled, Stinky stuck out his tongue, and sure enough, there was Tid holding on for dear life.

"Sol-ly," Stinky said with his tongue still hanging out. His eyes crossed as he tried to see little Tid. Stinky leaned down to let Tid slide off his tongue. Wet and weak-kneed, Tid was disgusted.

"Sorry," Stinky repeated, "I didn't see you."

"Didn't you ever hear 'look before you lick'?" Tid questioned as he dried himself off.

"No," admitted Stinky. "But I've heard 'look before you *leap*.' My dad has told me that a bunch of times."

"Ants don't leap," Bit stated briskly.

"Are . . . are you guys mad at me?" Stinky asked.

"Well, you almost ate me," Tid pointed out.

"But I said I was sorry," Stinky answered quietly, a tear in his eye.

"Excuse us for a moment,"
Tid said as he and Bit stepped
behind the onion bag to talk it over.

A few minutes later, Bit called up to
Stinky, "Sometimes you just need to give
people time to get over being scared and
angry." Bit paused and then added, "We
forgive you, but please be more careful. You're
not the only animal on the planet, you know."

"Are you guys animals?"

"Well, no. We're insects. But you have to be nice to everyone. Our mom said so."

"Everyone?" Stinky asked. "Even cats?"

"I'm pretty sure cats are on the Be-Nice list," Bit said, scratching his head.

Then Stinky questioned, "What about anteaters? Should we be nice to them?"

"Ooh, nooo, not them," Tid and Bit rang out at the same time.

"But *they're* animals," Stinky insisted.

"Yes, but they eat ants, silly mouse!"

"Well, cats eat mice, silly ants," Stinky said. "And if you haven't noticed, I'm a mice."

"Oh, dear," said Bit as he looked at Tid.

"Maybe we have to be nice to some folks from a distance," offered Tid.

"Maybe," said Bit, thinking. "But, how do we know who to be nice to?" asked Bit, now puzzled.

"I think you can tell by how someone looks if you should be nice," suggested Tid.

"I don't think so," said Stinky, "because Duff is a good-looking calico cat, but he'd eat me for lunch! And you can't tell how nice someone is by a present they offer you 'cause one time Duff left a piece of my favorite cheese on the floor, and when I leaned in to taste it, he tried to swat me with his paw!"

"Oh, Bit, remember when that well-dressed woodpecker told us he'd give us a ride to the top of the tree if we'd step out of our anthill?" Tid asked.

"That's right, Tid. Sooo, how do we know who to be nice to?" asked Bit, now even more puzzled than before.

"I think we ask our parents to help us make a Be-Nice list. They're more older and no anteaters or cats have eaten them yet, so they must know," announced Stinky.

"Good idea," agreed Tid and Bit, relieved to have an answer.

"Stinky?"

"Yes, Bit?"

"Did I ever tell you I was sorry for sticking you in the toe with that straw?"

"Nope."

"Well, I'm sorry. I just didn't know how else to get your attention before you swallowed Tid."

"I understand."

"Stinky?"

"Yes, Bit?"

"You're on our Be-Nice list, right at the top."

"Thank you, Tid and Bit, you're on *my* list too!"

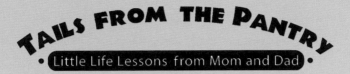

TAILS FROM THE PANTRY

· Little Life Lessons from Mom and Dad ·

SPUD

*O*nce upon a sack of potatoes sat a rat named Spud. Spud was feared throughout the house as the garage bully. And when he heard that there was a family of mice living in the pantry, Spud came dressed for troublemaking. He pulled on his meanest look, he squeezed into his beady-eyed stare, and he wiggled his voice into a growl.

What Spud didn't realize was that the MacKenzie mice had rigged up a string across the doorway of their pantry. When anyone stepped on the string, it rang a bell in the forgotten box of Christmas candy, high on the third shelf, where the mouse family lived. When the bell jingled in their living room, the mice would sneak a peek to see who was there.

"Oh my!" squealed Meatball to her brothers when she looked down and saw Spud. "It's a rat!"

Soccer and Stinky scampered to the window to see for themselves. Their parents had gone to the market and wouldn't be back until lunchtime.

"Take care of each other," Dad had reminded them as he and Mrs. MacKenzie headed out the door with the twins.

"Look, Stinky," whispered Soccer, "he's sniffing the air."

"What should we do?" Stinky asked his brother.

"Meatball, burrow into your room and stay there!" Soccer ordered. "Stinky, get our rubber bands and the bag of lima beans. And hurry!"

Within minutes, Stinky came back toting the rubber bands. "Where are the beans?" Soccer asked, keeping one eye on Spud.

"Well, I . . . uh . . . sorta ate them last night," Stinky confessed.

"Stinky!"

"Sorry."

"Well, we'd better think fast because Spud's headed in our direction!"

Spud was now on the first shelf. He was stacking up tuna fish cans to make stairs up to the second shelf.

"PSST, Soccer . . . PSST, Soccer," came a whisper from behind him.

"Meatball! I told you to burrow into your room!" Soccer said when he saw his sister's polka-dotted tail peeking out from behind the door.

"I know, Soccer, but I have something you need," Meatball promised.

"Not now, Sister, we're in danger!"

"But I have trinkets for your rubber bands!"

"What? Where?" Soccer turned around.

Meatball handed her shoebox of goodies to him.

"But, Meatball, this is your favorite collection. . . ."

"I know, but I think they'll work to keep us safe. Besides, what else do we have?"

Soccer knew that Meatball was right. He'd have to use them. The trinkets were treasures that Meatball had been collecting for a long time. There were buttons, a pink eraser, a cheese puff, gumdrops, miniature marshmallows, and her latest discovery, a ripe, juicy grape.

Loading up their trinkets and rubber bands, Soccer and Stinky marched up to the roof of their home to protect themselves. Suddenly there was a great roar as Spud jumped onto the third shelf. The loud noise so frightened the brothers that they dropped everything.

Spud laughed aloud, knowing he had the mice trapped. Soccer and Stinky backed up to the edge of the roof, their knees knocking. Then just as Spud leaned down to show the boys his pointy teeth, Meatball snuck up unnoticed and plopped on the grape, sending a spray of grape juice flying in Spud's direction.

Bull's-eye! She hit Spud right between his bushy eyebrows, causing him to stop and rub his wet face. The boys grabbed their rubber bands, reloaded, and let them fly.

ZAP! Soccer smacked the bully rat on the ear with a cheese puff.

ZING! Stinky hit Spud with a purple gumdrop.

"GRRRRR!" was Spud's reply.

Then Soccer thumped the bully with a spinning marshmallow, and Stinky got him with a yellow button. But before they could reload, Spud rushed toward the brothers and grabbed them. "You little pipsqueaks! I gotcha now!"

No sooner had Spud spoken than a pink, flying object bounced off the tip of his gnarly nose. Spud let out a mighty yelp and dropped the mice. He sat down with a thud. "My nose! My nose!" he howled. "Why'd you do that? I wasn't really gonna hurt nobody."

"Well, you sure did act like it!" Meatball announced. Soccer and Stinky turned to see who had rescued them. Meatball had pulled back a spoon, loaded it with the eraser, and flung it into the air.

"I was just—**SNIFF**—just trying to scare you guys—**SNIFF**." replied Spud.

"Well, you don't seem so scary now," Stinky teased.

"And you guys don't seem so little now," Spud admitted, getting up to walk away.

Spud's nose had swollen up to look like a Christmas tree light bulb. He stood up and headed down the shelves and back to the garage.

"Spud, just because we're smaller than you doesn't give you the right to be mean to us," Meatball began, throwing down a tissue to him. "Bullies aren't welcome here. When you learn to be kind, maybe you can come back and play with us."

As soon as their parents returned, Soccer, Stinky, and Meatball began talking all at once. "One at a time, please," instructed their dad.

So, taking turns, each mouse told what had taken place.

"Thank you for working together to send Spud on his way," Dad began, after hearing what had happened. "Standing up to a bully can be tough, but sometimes it's the only thing that helps."

"But, Daddy, I still felt sorry for Spud—even though I knew he was trying to scare us," Meatball said.

"I love your compassion, Meatball, but it's still good to be careful, especially when you don't trust someone," Dad explained.

"You know what else I learned, Dad?" Soccer added. "I learned girls can be as brave as boys." Soccer turned to his sister. "Thanks, Meatball. Stinky and I really needed your help."

"I'm so proud of all of you," Dad said with a smile. "Bullies can be big and scary, but remember, children: big is not about how tall you get, but how much you grow up on the inside."

Meatball was so happy, she ran to her room, put on her tutu, and spun around in circles. And inside, she felt herself growing up.

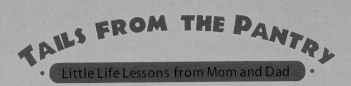

TAILS FROM THE PANTRY

Little Life Lessons from Mom and Dad

Basil and Parsley

Once upon a pantry shelf hid two mice, Basil and Parsley, the MacKenzie twins. They loved to play games with their brothers and sister—Soccer, Stinky, and Meatball. Today it was Stinky's turn to entertain the twins because Meatball and Soccer were helping their mom carry groceries to the third shelf of the pantry, where they lived in a forgotten box of Christmas candy.

"Ready or not, here I come!" teased Stinky.

"Okay, Stinky, come find us!" Basil called out as he slid behind a can of black pepper.

"Yes, we're ready, Stinky," chimed in Parsley, who was curled up behind a jar of ginger.

The twins giggled with excitement.

Basil and Parsley waited, and waited, and waited, but Stinky didn't come.

"What's taking so long?" whispered Parsley.

"I dunno. Yoo-hoo, Stinky, come find us," called Basil. But there was no answer.

"Where do you think Stinky is, Basil?" Parsley asked with a quiver in her voice. She was worried about their brother.

"He's probably looking somewhere else. I'm sure he'll be here any minute," Basil answered.

"That's silly, Basil! Stinky knows where we are because we *always* hide in the same place."

Basil's ears perked up. "Oh, wait, I think I hear Stinky now. Listen."

Parsley heard something, too. It sounded like three knocks and a squeak.

"I think Stinky is in trouble, Parsley," Basil whispered.

"Really? Why?" Parsley asked, wide-eyed.

"Well, remember the day Daddy told us about emergency signals? He said if we ever get into trouble, we should tap three times over and over to let someone know where we are."

Basil and Parsley listened again.

Tap, tap, tap—squeak.

"What should we do, Basil?"

"I don't know," Basil admitted.

Tap, tap, tap—squeak.

Tap, tap, tap—squeak.

"Well," Parsley insisted, "we have to do something. Stinky needs us."

Basil thought for a minute. "Look, Parsley, what if we take turns helping each other up onto the cans until we reach the next shelf? C'mon, I'll show you."

Basil knelt down. He told Parsley to stand on his back and then crawl up onto the can of tuna fish.

Parsley did what her brother said. "Now what?" she called down to Basil.

"Uh, I don't know. I can't jump that high without a boost," Basil confessed after trying several times.

"Why don't you nibble into that bag of marshmallows and roll one over to stand on."

"Good idea, Sister."

Basil nibbled away, and in no time he had made a hole big enough to pull out a marshmallow. He rolled it over to the tuna fish can; then he climbed onto it and pulled himself up beside Parsley.

Parsley stared up at the next can, which was even higher than the last. "Basil, how do we get up there?"

"Uh-oh, now *that's* a problem," Basil admitted.

Tap, tap, tap—squeak.

Tap, tap, tap—squeak.

"I know what we can do. Basil, go back down and get that empty mesh bag. Then nibble your way into that bag of spaghetti and hand up a few noodles. Oh, yes, and see those miniature marshmallows over there? Stick a couple of them in your pockets."

Basil went lickety-split and soon returned with the bag, the spaghetti, and the marshmallows. "Now what?" Basil huffed, out of breath from all the pulling and tugging.

"Well, we could throw the bag up in front of a can and scale it like rock climbers do."

Tap, tap, tap—squeak.

"C'mon, Sister, we've got to hurry!"

Parsley and Basil threaded the spaghetti strands through the open weave of the bag and then leaned it up against a can of corn.

"Okay, Parsley, you go first."

Parsley began scaling the bag. Higher and higher and higher she climbed, until she finally pulled herself up onto the can of corn. She peeked over the side to let Basil know she was safe, but looking down made her feel funny inside her tummy.

"I'm almost there," Basil called out, "but I need a hand to get up on the can."

"I can't look over the side, Basil. It makes the butterflies in my tummy flutter."

"Just hold out your hand and don't look down," Basil instructed. "When I grab your hand, pull as hard as you can." Parsley pulled hard until . . . *thump* . . . Basil was on the can beside her. They sat there together, looking at the shelf above their heads. Then Parsley began to cry. "Oh, Basil, what can we do? I'm so worried about Stinky!"

Basil thought and thought. Finally, it came to him. He pulled the marshmallows out of his pockets and tucked one under each foot.

"I really wanted to eat those marshmallows," Parsley confessed, "but it looks like you have a better idea."

Basil stood on his tippytoes, stretched his hands up to the edge of the shelf, and grabbed with all his might. But his hands slipped, and he tumbled back down and disappeared right over the edge of the shelf.

"Basil!" Parsley screamed.

Parsley peered over the scary edge. She couldn't believe her eyes. On the shelf below stood Spud the bully rat, holding Basil in his outstretched arms. Parsley didn't know if she should jump for joy or scream for help.

Then Spud did the nicest thing. Without a word, he put Basil on his shoulders and jumped onto the shelf where Parsley was. Now from Spud's shoulders, Basil safely stepped onto the next shelf. Spud helped Parsley do the same thing. After a stunned "Thank you!" from the twins, Spud tipped his baseball cap and headed back down, disappearing as quickly as he had come.

Basil and Parsley hugged. They couldn't believe Spud the bully had rescued them. Just then, they heard the taps again. They sounded much closer now.

Tap, tap, tap—squeak.

"Stinky? Stinky?" Parsley called.

"Here I am," Stinky called out. "Help me!"

The twins ran behind a pickle jar, and there was Stinky with the tip of his tail caught in a mousetrap.

"Oh, Stinky, how can we get you out of that mousetrap?" Basil asked.

"See that spoon over by the sugar bowl? You and Parsley will have to use it to pry open the metal piece that's holding my tail."

In a jiffy the twins pulled the spoon over and carefully slipped the tip of the spoon handle under the metal. They both hung on to the bowl of the spoon and pushed down as hard as they could, and finally the clamp moved just enough to free Stinky's tail.

Stinky gave the twins a big hug. "Boy, am I glad you found me," he said, holding his throbbing tail. "Let's go home."

At dinner that evening, Basil, Parsley, and Stinky shared their adventures with their family. Daddy asked them each to tell something they had learned that day. Basil was first.

"I learned that sometimes even a bully like Spud can be kind."

Parsley was next. "I learned that it's a lot easier to solve problems when we work together, like Basil and I did," she said.

Finally it was Stinky's turn. "Well, Dad, I learned that it's good to know how to signal for help when you're in trouble and also . . . that I'd rather be *part* of an adventurous tale than *lose* a tail!"